A Tree Place

To Kelly, who loves
poetry,
"Enjoy!"

Constance Levy 1999

Also by Constance Levy

I'M GOING TO PET A WORM TODAY
AND OTHER POEMS

A Tree Place
AND OTHER POEMS

CONSTANCE LEVY

illustrated by
ROBERT SABUDA

MARGARET K. McELDERRY BOOKS

Margaret K. McElderry Books
An imprint of Simon & Schuster
Children's Publishing Division
1230 Avenue of the Americas
New York, New York 10020

Designed by Nancy B. Williams
The text of this book is set in Baskerville.
The illustrations are rendered in pencil.

First Edition
Printed and bound in the United States of America
10 9 8 7 6 5 4 3

Library of Congress Cataloging-in-Publication Data
Levy, Constance.
A tree place and other poems / by Constance Levy ; illustrated by Robert Sabuda. — 1st ed.
p. cm.
Summary: A collection of forty poems about nature and the outdoor world.
ISBN 0-689-50599-X
1. Nature—Juvenile poetry.   2. Children's poetry, American.
1. Nature—Poetry.   2. American poetry.]   I. Sabuda, Robert, ill.   II. Title.
PS3562.E9256T73   1994   811'.54—dc20   93-20586

"Technique," © 1981 by Constance Levy, first appeared in the September 1981 issue of *Cricket*.

To M.D.L. and
Julie, Elana, Daniel, Sara, and Jonathan

CONTENTS

SURPRISES

I've learned that snakes
have cool silk skin
and earthworms shrink
when you're petting them,

that a butterfly frowns
as it dips and drinks
as if each sip
saps all its strength,

that early in a morning mist
a spider's web
is dew drop kissed,

that toads may look like
rocks with eyes,

and each new day
is a surprise...

An Orange-Lined Whelk

Once,
a sunset,
as it fell,
was caught
and kept
and hidden well
inside a twist
of ocean shell,
a knobby-knuckled
fist of brown.

And now the tide
has towed it in
and left it in the sand,
this shell that holds a sunset,
that I'm holding in my hand.

A SMALL EARTHQUAKE IN THE IVY

That small earthquake
in the ivy?
I see it, too,
but put your mind at ease.
It's just a scurrying
field mouse
passing through,
shivering the leaves,

a small gray visitor
underneath
on tangled vines
making leaf-waves
going by.
Do not disturb her;
she is wary of
most anything,
and very shy.

INCHWORM

A little green inchworm
dropped from a tree,
and rode in my hair
unknown to me,
till I looked in the mirror.
"Aha!" I said,
"What is this green thing on my head?"

And the worm must have wondered
seeing me,
"What is this funny looking tree?"

LITTLE BOATS

Little boats
at the dock,
weathered and gray,
you have worked all day.
Now play!
    Rock
    Roll with the ripples
    Bump together
    Have a romp
    Slap, slap, at waves
    Rap
    Glad-hand the water
    Dance and be happy!

TECHNIQUE

I watched a spider wrap her gnat
With such a flood of tidiness.
She twiddled all her nimble feet
And seemed to do a dance in place

While tying round a stream of thread
As pale and white as soft-spun milk,
So careful not to miss one step
Or spill a single
Drop
Of silk!

THE SWIMMER

The sun
underwater
makes chains of gold
that rearrange
as I reach through.
I feel at home
within this world
of sunlit water, cool and blue.
I sip the air;
I stroke;
I kick;
big bubbles bloom as I breathe out.
Although I have no tail or fin
I'm closer than I've ever been
to what fish feel
and think about.

MOON MAGIC

Summer night...
a brown moth
lies flat
on the back
door screen
moon bathing,
basking in silver.

Now this moth,
the color of tree bark
and old leather,
is silver as the moon,
as stars,
as a web of new dew.

How does a brown moth
turn so silver?
Is it the moon's magic?
Has it made *me* silver, too?

NOON SHADOWS

They've vanished from the grass:
from dogs,
trash cans,
benches,
trees,
me.
No ghost shapes to chase
or shadow tails
to tag along,
no fun.
Shadows are "out to lunch"
in the noontime sun.

Worm Warm

Earthworms
share their winter sleep
and hug together
way down deep,
deep down
beneath the ground you see
to keep warm
while it's wintery.

Their worm-warm balls
of hugging last
till all the shivery days
are past.
Though they don't show it
up above
I think worms need
a lot of love.

ICE TALK

Listen,
ice words
in the trees:
crisp pops,
fire-crackles,
ticks and clicks
like bug talk
in summer weeds,
small sounds that grow
in the silence of snow.

Who answers?
Only your footsteps
and your breath-huffs
and the wing beats
of a passing crow.

DANDELION ROOTS

Dandelion roots,
are muscle and lace
and mean to stay,
burrowing down
in soft spring soil,
anchoring deep,
getting a good grip
underneath,
offering earthworms
a ladder to climb
after their long
winter's sleep.

THE PELICANS

The pelicans
set their sights,
then break through
sun-sparked ripples
in a flash,
crash-diving
from great heights,

filling their pouches
with batches
of fish.

Those pelicans
have a knack
for fishing,
a kind of
surprise attack
for fishing.

I wish
I could fish
like that.

S Is for Snake

Quick as a blink;
too swift
for me to think,
that slim black snake
raked its initial
in the dust
under my next step,
crossing through it
almost before I knew it
    scribbling:
    S is for snake
    S is for snake
How did he learn
to do it?

HIDE-AND-SEEK

It's hide and seek.
I climb a tree
and from a leafy limb
I watch my seeker seeking me
and sneak a look at him.

The trunk is strong
to lean upon.
The leaves leave room to peek.
If it had apples for me, too,
I'd stay up here a week.

POWER FAILURE

Greedy lightning
struck:
lashed its wild
tail
with a crash,
lunged and raged,
stung
the sky's dark skin,
drawing blood.
"More!" it ranted,
"More!
"I want it all tonight!"
A louder crash…its tongue
licked down
and stole my light.

MOON PEACH

This autumn moon
is very near
and seems within our reach,
a luscious gold
enormous sphere,
a ripe and mammoth peach.

Not like the moons
of silver white
as distant as the stars,
but close enough to taste, almost,
and make us feel
it's ours.

GREENSWEET

There's a mower roving over
summer's crop, nonstop;
carving rows,
clipping tufts,
stirring clover,

opening each blade and stem
to free its hidden spice,
mixing all the
greensweet scents:
minty, herby,
nice!

The air is rich with summer now.
Breathe deeply—can't you tell?
If Mother Nature wore perfume
this is how she'd smell!

THE GLEAM TEAM

One evening on an ivy leaf
two fireflies who met
decided they would like to do
a little light duet.
And for an hour or so they glowed
a double dip of glimmer,
which left the other fire-fliers
looking watts, watts dimmer.

THE THREE OF US

A rabbit in the tall grass
chewing a stem
stops chewing.

A black cat
stalking mice
stops what he is doing.

And the three of us
who have never met,
together, are watching
the gold sun set.

A Tree Place

It's quite a cozy place to live
when leaves are dense and secretive
and swish in hushes whisper soft.
A tree is such a private loft.

Of course, sometimes you have to share
your tree place with the squirrels upstairs
who drop their nutshells in your hair.

And ants will visit, probably,
all over you, as they do me,
in places ants ought not to be
and, well, there goes your privacy!

ON THE BRIDGE AT THE JAPANESE GARDEN

Fish of every color
in a splashy flashy show
gathering to catch the bits
of fish food that we throw.

Jostling acrobatic carp
jumbled in a bunch
in and out and underneath
eager for some lunch.

Even some on tippy-tails
mouths so opened wide
we can toss the food to them
right straight down inside.

VOLCANO

If you were a volcano,
asleep in the same spot
for a hundred years,
with old anger
rumbling and burning
your insides

wouldn't you awake
screaming with fire,
spitting rocks and ashes,
throwing a flaming fit
not caring who or what
you hit?

LET'S POP THE CORN

Let's pop the corn
and fire the logs
and take off our shoes
and wiggle our toes
and sit on the rug
and talk.
Let's eat all the popcorn
and pop some more,
and do again
what we did before.

They fit:
the popcorn, the fire
the pops and crackles
the flickers and crunches
the wiggles
the warmth
the winter weather
and nice
soft
talking
together.

FOR RENT: ONE MOON SNAIL SHELL

FOR RENT beside the ocean's shore:
One cozy, well kept
Moon Snail shell.
No snail resides there
Anymore.
(It left and didn't close the door.)

A homeless hermit crab came by.
The shell FOR RENT sign
caught his eye.
He gave the Moon Snail shell a try.

He folded in, umbrella style
and said, "I'll stay in here awhile."

You see, a turtle comes with shell,
a moon snail builds one very well,
but hermit crab lives by his wits
and has to *find* a shell that fits!

SEED SECRETS

Seeds,
small as grains of sand,
conspired with the earth
in deep dark places,
secretly sipping,
sipping,
stretching,
anchoring
and hankering for
up;
now they break to the light
like rows of green
periscopes
sneaking their first
look.

ROCK TUMBLER

This rock tumbler
takes a load
of ordinary stones,
craggy and coated with
years of grime,
and churns them
for weeks at a time,
pebble-smacking,
click-clacking,
clunking like dancing bones.

It hums, drones.
The rocks talk
rock-talk
and bathe in gray grit
to smooth their crags,
polish themselves sleek
and bright,
to look fit.

A rock tumbler
is a beauty parlor
for stones,
isn't it?

HUMMINGBIRD WITH RED
(archilochus colubris)

A bright, slight
sleek-as-a-pear
glitter-green bird
hangs from the air

quenching his thirst
from red to red
as he hovers over
the flower bed

with red on his bib
as if he has spilled
some flower juice
he sips his fill

through a secret tongue
in his slender bill.

Drizzle

One drop
surprised my nose—
a splat,
silent and soft
as the kiss of a gnat.
I wondered,
"Sky, will you send more,
or leave it at that?"

Two drops,
two splats,
a *pitter-pat*
and from the trees
a sort of *sizzle*...
Sky very quickly answered back.
Now I am all kissed up with drizzle!

THE PRINCESS OF FOOT

The sole of my foot
is a princess,
an incredibly sensitive child.
This tidbit of gravel
that slipped in my shoe,
as usual, is driving her wild.

It's the same for a rock
or a lump in my sock,
or a seed or a twig—
she screams, "PAIN!"
And if I don't stop
and remove it at once
she'll complain
and complain
and complain!

I've told her that life
can't always be
plush carpets,
soft grasses
and fur,
but the Princess of Foot
is as stubborn as stone
and there's no use
in talking to her.

MORNING IS BUSY

Morning is busy
with treetops to dust,
white clouds to fluff up
and colors that must
be lightened and brightened:
the red of the rose,
the green grass, the orange sun
to rub till it glows,
changing a world that's drab and hazy
letting the rest of the day be lazy.

So deftly it does it,
so loving its touch,
I think that's why I like
the morning so much.

Flower Feelings

Little yellow flower
does it tickle,
do you itch
when a butterfly is
straddling your petals
as it sips?
Do you wish you could scratch
or give a little twitch?

When that quick-draw straw
plunges nearly to your stem
does it sting like the jab
of a needle or a pin?
Would you scream, "Bug, off!"
If not that
what, then?

ONCE IN AN EARLY MORNING MIST

Once in an early morning mist
I splashed my dewy way along
to where upon a holly tree
a spider's sparkling harp was strung

and in the soft and silver light
I blew a breath across the strings
and suddenly—a symphony
of little dew notes, shimmering!

MERGE

Construction ahead—
The sign says MERGE.
The lanes converge,
and every car and truck and van
has to wait until the man
signals them to go on through.
      There's
      one
      lane
      now
    where there
    were two.
They wait.
Then one by one they pass
like grains of sand
in an hourglass.
While further back
the traffic's fat
and s..l..o..w
and itching to go!

CAMOUFLAGED AMPHIBIAN

A gray rock
hops
across the road.
It stops
and looks surprised.

It blinks two
little polka dots
that look a lot
like eyes,

but I can spot
this camouflaged
amphibian's
disguise.

I know his tricks;
when I come near
he'll hop away
and disappear,

and make me search
for him in clumps
of scratchy grass,
then leave me stumped!

And after that
I'll look for eyes
all day
along the road,
inspecting any rock with dots
to see if it's
that toad!

To a Cicada of Four Surprises

You surprised me first
as you sat in my palm.
I thought you'd be jumpy
but you seemed quite calm.

Your back was as dark
as green can be,
like a piece of the shadow
deep in your tree.
But your tummy was white
and soft as a rug,

and you felt very heavy,
I thought, for a bug.

Then when you sprang
as you shrieked
KEREEEEEEEE!
all the way in one jump
to your own home tree
I wondered—
were you as surprised with me?

A Cicada Story

He spent the winter
when he was new
under the tree
where he dug a place,
and sipped root beer
until he grew.
(Well, it *was* root juice,
and that's the truth!)

Now he sits in the tree
playing tummy-tunes
with a bunch of the guys
this afternoon
trying to be a real cool bug
with his long, strong song.

Want to hum along?

WASP ON THE WEEDSTALK

Pokes a leaf on top
peeks under
pokes again
buzzes at a knob
circumnavigates the stem.

Whipping through the air
looking stern and tough
returns to poke again;
two pokes was not enough.

A wasp inspects the world:
the undersides of things,
the crevices and cracks,
the doors and window screens

and though I fear its wrath,
wasp work looks interesting.

WHITE DANDELION

One puff of breath
is enough,
and this white dandelion
erupts
into a snow of fluff
brief as a laugh,
dusting the air with
great spring stuff!

FOREST SECRETS

The forest talks
The forest sings,
Snapping twigs
Brushing wings.
Doves are cooing,
Owls are whooing,
But I can't see
Who's doing things.

The forest talks.
The forest sings.
The underbrush is
Rustling
From some small creature's feet,
I'm sure,
But I can't find
The rustle-er.

Secrets make good listening
When forests talk,
When forests sing.